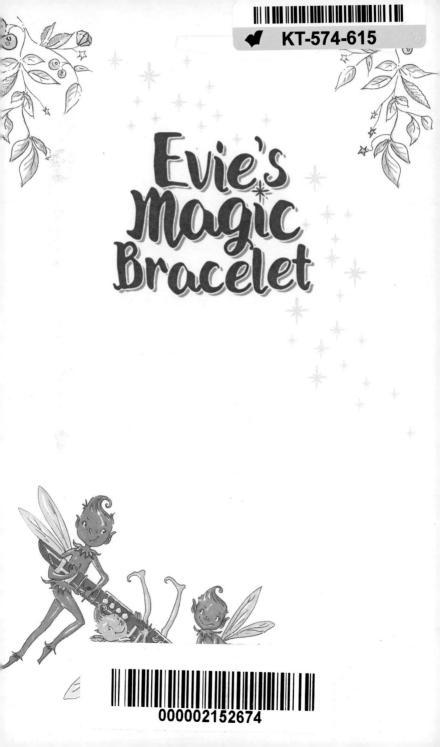

Evie's Magic Bracelet

Read more in the Evie's Magic Bracelet series!

1. The Silver Unicorn

2. The Enchanted Puppy

3. The Sprites' Den

4. The Unicorn's Foal

5. The Clocktower Charm

6. The Fire Bird

7. The Golden Sands

Evie's Magic Bracelet

The Clocktower Charm

JESSICA ENNIS-HILL
and Elen Caldecott

**Illustrated by
Erica-Jane Waters**

Hodder
Children's
Books

HODDER CHILDREN'S BOOKS

First published in Great Britain in 2018 by Hodder and Stoughton

1 3 5 7 9 10 8 6 4 2

Text and illustrations copyright © Jessica Ennis Limited, 2018

The moral right of the author has been asserted.

A CIP catalogue record for this book
is available from the British Library.

ISBN 978 1 444 93443 4

Printed and bound in Great Britain
by Clays Ltd, St Ives plc

The paper and board used in this book
are made from wood from responsible sources

MIX
Paper from
responsible sources
FSC

To Charlotte x
– J.E-H.

To Lily, by herself
– E.C.

Chapter 1

Evie Hall was singing at the top of her voice and the crowd was going wild.

Her eyes were screwed shut. She held the microphone to her lips as she blasted the chorus to the very back of the arena. 'Do you neeeed anyone?!' she sang. 'Oh yeah, neeeeed anyone to love?!' Thousands of

fans whooped and hollered.

Then she opened her eyes and laughed.

Her stage was the bathroom mirror. Her
adoring fans were really a colourful crowd

of toothbrushes in a mug. Her microphone was a comb. She pulled it through her hair. Above her head magic swirled in a golden cloud. She grinned and Evie-in-the-mirror grinned too. She couldn't imagine ever feeling brave enough to sing in front of a crowd, but it was fun to do it in her imagination.

'Evie, shake a leg!' Dad shouted from the bottom of the stairs.

'Two ticks,' Evie replied. She put her comb/microphone down and watched the bursts of happy magic twinkle and fade.

The magic had started when Grandma Iris sent Evie a bracelet that let her talk to animals. It was only supposed to last for three days, but a meeting with a friendly unicorn meant that Evie and her friends, Ryan and Isabelle, could see magic all the time, even if they could only use it with Grandma Iris' help. Luckily, Grandma Iris had sent lots of bracelets, so there had been plenty of brilliant adventures.

Evie tugged back her dark hair and slipped on a bobble. She was ready for the school day. With one last yelled chorus, she headed downstairs.

As she passed the front door, there was a smart knock. 'I'll get it!' Evie yelled in Dad's general direction. She opened the door to see the postman standing on the doorstep.

Morning, Evie pet,' he said with a warm

smile. 'Another one of those interesting parcels you get. Here you go.' He rummaged in his big, red bag until he found the parcel. It was wrapped in bright paper, and tied with a ribbon, and Evie recognised it immediately. 'It's from Grandma Iris!' she said, in delight.

The postie tapped the brim of his baseball cap. 'I'd best get on,' he said. 'It looks like rain!'

Evie peered out. There were tarmac grey clouds above their house, but she didn't mind – a bit of rain wasn't enough to dampen her spirits on a bracelet day! 'Thank you!' she said, and closed the door.

Evie rushed to the front room, her heart

pounding. What magic had Grandma Iris sent this time? She pulled off the wrapping and lifted the lid. Inside the box was a beautiful blue bracelet. Ribbons weaved around sapphire-coloured beads like waves. Before putting it on, Evie checked the box for a note from Grandma Iris. She usually couldn't make head nor tail of Grandma Iris' riddles, but it was nice to try and guess. The note, with Grandma's riddle, was buried under tissue paper:

What goes up must come down,
Unless there's magic in your town!
You'll make a splash, I've no doubt,
once the bracelet's turned about.

Hmm. Evie slipped her hand through the bracelet and pulled the sleeve of her school shirt down over it. The last line of the riddle made sense – it was turning the bracelet three times that activated the magic; she'd found that out before. She wasn't so clear about the first line though. 'What goes up must come down.' Was it something to do with flying, or jumping?

The only way to find out for sure would be to turn the bracelet three times, then she'd see what it could do. Was there enough time before she had to leave for school?

Evie eyed the door. She could hear Dad and Lily in the living room, mithering over clearing the breakfast pots. Lily wasn't very

good at helping out when she was asked, so it could take a while. She had time!

Evie pushed back her sleeve, and turned the bracelet once, twice, three times and …

… absolutely nothing happened.

Evie spun around on her heel. Was the furniture floating up to the ceiling? Was she able to bounce really high? She jumped up and down a few times to see. But no, she came back down with a thump.

'Evie!' Mum's voice shouted from the hallway. 'What are you up to in there? It sounds like a herd of elephants.'

'Nothing!' Evie called back.

Evie sighed, and tidied away the parcel and its wrapping. She didn't know what the bracelet did, but she was sure that Grandma Iris wouldn't let her down. She was just going to have to wait and find out.

Ten minutes later Evie, Lily and Dad all tumbled out of the house, with Mum calling instructions after them: 'Have you got your butty boxes? Lily, did you get the signed permission slip? Wait! Umbrellas! You'll need an umbrella.'

Dad chuckled. 'Wait here, girls,' he said, then trotted back to the door to collect the umbrella Mum was holding out. He gave her a peck on the cheek. 'Have a great day, love,' he told her.

They walked to the end of the road and turned on to the bustling High Street where full buses trundled past crammed with people on the way to work. A cold breeze blew and it wasn't long before the first drops of rain splashed down. Evie tucked her chin into her scarf. Dad popped up the big umbrella. The drops became a drizzle, then a downpour, drumming on the top of the brolly.

Lily squealed. She hadn't quite grown out of jumping in puddles, but without wellies it was too splashy. The rain was so heavy it bounced back up and splattered their shoes and socks.

'Come closer, girls,' Dad said, 'it's raining cats and dogs.' He crouched so that they were all sheltered.

'Rain, rain go away, come again another day,' Lily sang.

Evie agreed. She was going to have damp shoes and wet socks all day. Yuck! She wished it would stop! And, with that thought, gold light swirled and twinkled around her wrist. Magic was twirling out of her bracelet! It was waking up. The magic swelled, and became a golden halo spreading out around all three of them. Evie cast nervous glances at Dad and Lily. Had they noticed?

But no, it was only Evie who could see what was happening.

As they walked down the street, the magic was sheltering them from the rain, like a giant, golden bubble. The drumming sound on the umbrella stopped. The magic pushed water aside on the pavement, forcing it to form little streams that ran into the gutter.

Evie remembered Grandma Iris' riddle:

'You'll make a splash' it had said. She watched the water on the ground race away from her feet as she stepped. She'd worked out what the bracelet could do – it controlled water. Cool!

But Dad had stopped walking. He lowered the umbrella.

No rain fell on them, but he could see rain falling all around him. He lifted the umbrella, then lowered it, lifted it, lowered it. 'What on earth ...' Dad muttered.

Oh cripes! He couldn't see the magic, but he could definitely see the result!

I wish it would rain, Evie thought fiercely. As soon as the words formed in her mind, the magic zipped back into a small ball and

13

swirled back into the bracelet, as though it had been hoovered up.

Rain crashed down on to Dad's upturned face. He spluttered and whipped the umbrella back above them. 'Sorry, girls,' he said, 'I thought it had stopped. Hurry!'

They walked as quickly as they could to school, down the busy High Street where car wipers flicked back and forth and shop windows misted up inside. Soon Starrow Juniors was in sight, and Evie felt lucky she hadn't given the magical game away!

Chapter 2

Isabelle was waiting impatiently for Evie just inside the school door.

'You'll never guess, you'll never guess!' Isabelle said. Her hair was loose today and it bounced up and down with her eagerness.

'Can I dry off a minute?' Evie said. She dripped on to the welcome mat. Dad's

15

umbrella hadn't held off the sideways rain!

'No,' Isabelle said. 'This is important. Just shake for a bit.'

Evie grinned. 'I can do better than that.' She showed Isabelle the bracelet on her wrist.

'Ooh, what does it do?' Isabelle asked.

'Watch.' Evie turned the bracelet, then wished, 'Rain, get off me!'

The drips flew off her in all directions, like a water firework exploding. The spray hit the door behind her … and Isabelle who was standing in front of her.

'Hey!' Isabelle wiped the drips from her face with her sleeve.

'Oops, sorry. It controls water. Or, at

16

least, that's what I was trying to make it do,' Evie said.

'It's all right. I don't mind getting splashed by magic.'

Evie slipped her hand through Isabelle's arm and they headed together towards their classroom. 'So, what was the exciting thing you wanted to tell me?'

'Oh yes.' Isabelle skipped up and down. 'You'll never guess. The auditions are today!'

Evie felt her excitement drain away like water down a plughole. 'Auditions?' she asked doubtfully.

'Yes. Miss Williams put the posters up this morning. The school are putting on a show. A musical!'

Evie felt more wilted than overboiled cabbage. It was one thing to sing at her reflection, but singing, on stage, in front of rows and rows of people, all looking at her, that was another kettle of fish!

She'd had actual nightmares about just that. More than once. But Isabelle was looking at her with a huge smile and a shining face. Obviously, the idea was like all her birthdays and Christmases rolled into one. 'I'm going to audition for the lead role. And first clarinet in the orchestra. And star dancer. What about you?'

Evie wondered whether she might audition for the role of helping-out-backstage-where-no-one-would-see-her. She didn't say so,

18

though. Instead, she asked, 'What sort of thing can I do?'

'Come and see.' Isabelle dragged Evie to a noticeboard outside the Year 6 classroom. On it was one of the posters that Miss Williams had put around the school. It said:

BE A FRIEND

MUSICAL AUDITIONS

TODAY AT MORNING BREAK
COME TO THE MUSIC CORRIDOR,

**READY TO SING,
OR DANCE,
OR PLAY
AN INSTRUMENT.**

JOIN A CLUB!

NOTICES:

All those capital letters looked a bit too shouty to Evie. She didn't feel ready to sing or dance or play an instrument. Perhaps she could pretend to have lost her voice? Or caught a cold in the rain? Or twisted her ankle?

She trudged into class and sat down at her desk with a sigh.

Miss Williams, their teacher, came into the classroom looking serious. She put her bag-for-life stuffed full of books and papers under her chair and turned to look at the class.

'Year 6,' she said. 'I've just heard something very worrying. It seems that the school caretaker was on the roof, clearing

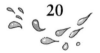

20

the gutters, when he distinctly heard the sound of children messing about in the clock tower. I have to tell you that no one is to go roaming around up there. It's dangerous. The walkways on the roof are for adults only. It isn't a playground and you have a perfectly good yard to use. Is that clear? Now, where's the whiteboard rubber?'

Evie's desk was beside the window. She looked out. Starrow Juniors was an old Victorian school. The main building had a clock tower balanced right in the middle of the roof, with a ladder that led down to a narrow walkway. Under the dark, rainy sky the tower looked like a huge finger raised to tell her off. The chimney stacks at either end of the roof were like castle turrets glowering above her. Would anyone really want to go and play up there? It looked scary.

With the auditions looming, she already had one absolutely terrifying thing to worry about. She definitely wouldn't be going near the clock tower.

Evie spent the morning barely listening to Miss Williams and the history project they were meant to be working on. All she could think about was break time and the auditions. It was fine for Isabelle. She loved being the centre of attention, and could sing and dance and play the clarinet – more or less. But it was different for Evie. She got so nervous whenever she had to do anything in

front of a crowd. Even getting up to read in
front of Year 6 was bad enough.

The bell for break rang all too quickly.

'Come on,' Isabelle said. 'Today it's the
school play, but tomorrow – superstardom!'
Isabelle yanked her out of her chair and
tugged her down to the music corridor,
where the auditions were going to happen.
Ryan was right behind them. He didn't mind

whether he got a lead role or not, he just
wanted to have fun.

Evie's palms were sweaty. Her heart
pounded in her ears, just standing in front
of the door. There were already a few people
there before them, and Mr Khan, the music
teacher, called them into his room, one by
one. Waiting outside, in the flickering strip
light, Evie felt weak and shaky. Someone
was singing beautifully inside the room,
a folk song they'd learned last term. It
was amazing. She couldn't sing like that
in a month of Sundays. Her throat felt as
dry and squeezed as a camel in an airing
cupboard. This was impossible.

'Are you all right?' Ryan asked.

'I think I'm just going to go to the bathroom for a minute,' Evie gasped. She hurtled away from the queue and slammed into the nearest girls' bathroom. The white tiles and smell of cleaner made her think of a hospital room. She could never go through with this. She turned on a tap and let it run over her hands. She splashed the cold water on her face.

She wished that the auditions were cancelled.

As soon as the words formed in her mind, gold magic swirled and danced from her bracelet.

Uh-oh.

The magic bobbed and twirled towards

the taps. What was it doing? Evie tried
to grab it … but her hands passed right
through. The magic touched the taps. The
trickle of water surged. It splashed and
gurgled into the basin.

Then the next tap burst on, and then
the next.

Evie turned the tap, but it just spun
around and around in her hand. The
water poured like a waterfall. The basins
couldn't cope. They were full in seconds,
then overflowing. Water splashed to the
floor, soaking her shoes. It was a cascade,
a torrent.

There was water roaring everywhere.

The door to the bathroom slammed open.

'What is that awful noise?' Miss Williams stood in the doorway. A wave of water flowed over her shoes into the corridor beyond. Her mouth dropped open.

'Evie Hall, what on earth have you done?' Miss Williams said.

Chapter 3

The water swished past Miss Williams and surged out into the corridor. Evie spun the taps wildly, but that did absolutely nothing to stop the flood.

Magic! It was magic that had done this, because she'd wished for the auditions to be cancelled. The water was still rising.

Miss Williams waded across the bathroom, splashing through to reach the big red tap on the far wall that controlled the flow of water to the sinks. With a few smart turns, she cut the water supply. In moments, the torrent was back to a trickle. Then it was just a few lone drips plopping into the basin.

Phew.

There was still water on the floor, right out into the corridor. Evie sloshed through to see how bad it was. The water had run under the classroom doors. The middle of the corridor was practically a river. The people in the queue to audition were all ankle-deep in the deluge. She hung her head. This was her fault. And she couldn't even use magic to clear up without Miss Williams getting suspicious.

She turned to look at her teacher. 'I'm sorry,' Evie whispered. 'I didn't meant to turn on all the taps. It just sort of happened.'

'I'm not angry,' Miss Williams said, very, very angrily, 'I'm disappointed. I expected you to be more sensible. Go and fetch a mop. Once this is all cleaned up, we'll be having a very serious conversation. Is that clear?'

Evie hadn't expected the day to get worse, but Miss Williams clearly thought it could.

She traipsed to the cleaner's store and asked to borrow a mop and bucket. But by the time she got back to the music corridor, the water had soaked into the carpet and there were just puddles left to make her feel guilty.

She mopped them up. She wasn't going to use magic. It wasn't right. She'd made the mess and she had to clean it up properly.

Evie was pushing the mop through a puddle so big it was practically a pond with fish in, when she heard stomps and splashes behind her as someone approached. Isabelle. And she was looking very cross indeed.

'The auditions are cancelled!' she said. 'The classroom is too wet. Mr Khan has gone to get a big hairdryer.'

'A big hairdryer?' Evie had never heard of that.

'Well, a dehumidi-something. Basically a machine to clean up the massive mess you made. Why did you go and soak the school?' Isabelle's eyebrows were pulled tight together in fury.

Evie kept her eyes on the mop. She pushed its grey strands across the floor, making ripples on the indoor-pond. She realised her eyes were a bit damp too. 'I didn't mean to,' she said. 'I was just thinking about how much I wanted the auditions not to happen, and well, I got my wish. Magic did it.'

'But you're in charge of the magic!'
Isabelle insisted.

Was she? She didn't feel in charge. She
felt small and silly and she was left pushing
a mop around while everyone was cross
with her.

'I'm sorry,' Evie said sadly.

Isabelle huffed. She turned and marched
off, sploshing and swinging her arms as
she went.

Evie felt a tear roll down her cheek. Isabelle
was right to be angry. She'd ruined the show.

'Budge over,' Isabelle's voice said moments
later. Evie looked. Isabelle was back, holding
a second mop. Ryan was behind her too, with

a handful of old rags and a bucket. They'd come to help.

Evie could have hugged them both, but she was a bit damp and drippy and they probably wouldn't like it. So, she just budged over and let them help. Soon the corridor was looking less like a lake and more like a school again.

'Thanks,' Evie said when they were done. 'I'm sorry again about the auditions.'

Isabelle nudged her with her shoulder. 'It's all right. What are besties for? And anyway, the auditions aren't *cancelled* cancelled. They're postponed until the end of the day. So we can all have another chance.'

Oh.

The auditions were still on. She was still

35

going to have to get up in front of everyone
and sing, or dance, or just have them *looking*
at her.

Ryan must have guessed what she was
thinking. 'It isn't that bad,' he said. 'You can
join the choir, or the orchestra. You don't
have to do a solo or anything.'

'I don't?' Evie asked hopefully.

'Well,' Ryan said. 'You have to audition by yourself, *obviously*. But once you've done that, you can hide in the crowd.'

Oh. Again.

As she wrung out her mop one last time, Evie wondered if she could hide from the auditions completely? Maybe sneak under her desk until everyone had gone home? She didn't have to audition.

'You totally have to audition,' Isabelle said, slipping her arm through Evie's. 'I was going to play the clarinet, but I've put it down somewhere and now I can't find it. So, I'm definitely going to sing instead. It will be so cool for the three of us to perform together. We could be a quartet!'

37

'I think there are four people in a quartet,' Ryan said.

'We'll be a three-tet, then. We can be the stars of the show.'

They wandered back to the cleaner's store. Isabelle was clearly imagining strutting her stuff on stage. She skipped along, singing into the mop like it was a microphone. The charm bracelet she was wearing on her wrist jangled in time.

There was no way that Evie was going to get out of this.

But she couldn't imagine any way that she could do it either. She was too scared, utterly, completely and disastrously terrified.

She didn't know what she was going to do.

Chapter 4

Evie stood, feeling very sorry for herself, while Miss Williams gave her the promised telling-off. They were outside the classroom. Evie kept her eyes on the criss-crossed wooden floor while Miss Williams talked about responsibility and thoughtfulness. Evie's tummy wriggled in shame.

'I know auditions can be stressful, which is why we'll say no more about it,' Miss Williams said. 'But I don't want any repeat of this behaviour. If you feel worried, you talk to me about it. Don't act out like a toddler.'

Evie nodded miserably. Miss Williams thought she was babyish. And she was right – Evie was scared of everything. She sloped back into the classroom and flopped down at her desk.

She did her very best to listen to the lesson, but it was difficult. The audition was like a big, black storm cloud scudding over and ruining everything. The more Evie wanted the day to drag, the more

40

it seemed to gallop past.

It seemed like no time before the bell rang for dinner.

Ryan and Isabelle charged out into the playground after eating. Evie followed behind.

'What's the matter?' Isabelle asked. 'Are you still moping about mopping?'

Evie shrugged. 'Not that exactly.'

'What then?' Ryan asked. The air was damp with drizzle and they sheltered near the garden hut. Ryan hopped up on to the side of one of the big planters and swung his legs from side to side. 'Is something else bothering you?'

Evie wanted to tell them. They were her

besties, after all. Isabelle had said so. It was just that Isabelle was so dramatic and so full of beans that she'd probably never been nervous in her life. And Ryan was so relaxed that nothing seemed to bother him.

'Tell us,' Isabelle said.

Evie bit her lip. 'You'll think I'm silly. I am silly.'

'Give over,' Ryan protested. 'Tell us.'

'It's just,' Evie began, 'it's just when I think about the auditions, it makes me want to dig a really deep hole, right the way to Australia, and jump down inside and never come out.' She stared at the planters with their little lime-green seedlings.

'Why?' Isabelle said.

Evie felt her cheeks redden. 'I'm not brave like you,' she whispered.

Isabelle guffawed. 'You? Of course you are. Don't be daft.'

'I'm not,' Evie insisted. 'You should have heard my heart thump this morning. It was like a brass band on May Day – and that was just from standing in the corridor.

43

I wasn't even doing the audition.'

Ryan leapt down and turned to look right at her. 'Evie Hall, we both know how brave you are because you've proved it to us in all our adventures.'

Evie shook her head. She hadn't, not really. She'd never done anything she was really scared by – all the things they'd got up to together she'd done because they were fun.

She looked up, embarrassed by Ryan's stare. Her gaze landed on the clock tower. It looked more menacing than ever. It was built of dark red bricks and black slate. There was one clock face that gleamed white as bone while the dark hands ticked the time. Above the clock face was a small window that reflected the grey sky. It looked like something from a ghost story. It was odd that there was a whole bit of the school that she'd never been to, never explored. Why weren't children allowed up there?

A tiny idea started to form in Evie's mind.

'You don't have to prove anything to anyone. I'm not even sure I want to audition, actually,' Ryan was saying.

But Evie kept looking at the dark tower.

Isabelle giggled. 'What's the matter, Ryan? Are you scared?'

'No. Not really. Hardly at all,' Ryan said.

'Scaredy-cat!' Isabelle teased.

Ryan leapt towards her, more like a

lion than a scaredy-cat. She shrieked and ran from his grip. He gave chase, and the two of them weaved between the planters, whooping and shrieking.

But Evie didn't join in. Her idea was starting to take shape. 'I could go into the clock tower,' she whispered. 'It's super scary. And out of bounds, for some mysterious reason. Hey!' she called.

The idea fizzed inside her, bursting into life. It was brilliant! Miss Williams had said it was dangerous, but the caretaker went up there all the time. If she explored the tower, and got back down safely, then that proved she was brave. She'd have to make sure no one saw her. After Miss Williams had expressly said that they weren't to go there, she'd be in big trouble. Her heart fluttered at the thought of Miss Williams' epic telling-off ability. But that was what made it so perfect. If she could do it, despite feeling scared, then it definitely proved she wasn't a scaredy-cat.

'Hey!' Evie said, a little louder. 'I'm going up there,' she said firmly.

Isabelle and Ryan, both a little out of breath, stopped chasing each other.

'Up where?' Ryan asked.

'To the clock tower. To prove I'm brave.'

'I've always wanted to go up there!' Isabelle said. 'I wonder which kids have been exploring? I wish they'd invited us. When will we go? Now? There's still half an hour of dinner time left.'

Evie shook her head. 'No. Not us. Just me. I'm doing it alone.'

Ryan frowned, his face full of concern. 'Evie, you're one of the bravest people I know. What about the time we defended your grandpa's garden from sprites? Or that time when you and Isabelle saved me from an angry unicorn?'

Grey clouds scudded across the sky, threatening heavier rain. Evie pulled her coat tighter. It was cold enough to need a scarf, but she'd lost hers somewhere. 'It wasn't just me, was it?' she said. 'You two were with me all of those times. I'm frightened that on my own I'm just a quivering wreck.'

Isabelle nudged her gently. 'But we're all always better together. It doesn't mean we're no good on our own. Anyway. There's no way at all that I'm letting you go and poke around in a spooky clock tower by yourself. It sounds like too much fun. What if you find a ghost?'

Evie dithered for a second. Was it better to

go on her own, or with her friends? Isabelle's smile and twinkling eyes decided it for her. She would let them come, but she'd go up there first. And she would be on the watch for any chance to be brave – she couldn't let herself down twice in one day.

'How do we get to the clock tower?' Evie asked.

'We just need to go through a door on the upper floor. I know where it is,' Isabelle said. 'There's just one teensy tiny problem.'

'Which is?' Ryan asked.

'The door is kept locked. And the key is kept in the staff room.'

Chapter
5

If Evie was going to prove to herself that
she really was brave, then she was going
to have to sneak the key to the clock tower
from underneath the eagle eyes of all of the
teachers. Somehow.

'We need a distraction,' Isabelle said.

'Like a flood?' Ryan suggested hopefully.

51

'No!' Evie insisted. 'There've been enough floods here for one day, thank you very much. I don't want to ruin the school.'

'Let's check it out and see if we can think of a plan,' Isabelle said. She led the way across the busy school yard and into the main building. The sounds of the yard echoed in the corridors – whoops and yells and laughter – but there was no one around indoors. 'This way.' Isabelle took them to the narrow staircase that wound up towards the first-floor attics. The staff room was nestled up there, far away from the din of the school. They crept up, trying not to make the stairs creak.

At the top of the creaky staircase there

was a short corridor. The walls were cream and the three doors that led off it were a dark, ivy green. One door opened on to the staff room, the next was a bathroom and the last was the door that led up to the clock tower. It had a huge, old-fashioned keyhole, like a mouth yawning. Evie slipped nearer, on tiptoes, and turned the handle, but the door was locked shut.

The door to the staff room was slightly ajar. A gentle hubbub of chatter drifted out. The air smelled of coffee and perfume. Evie crouched down low and spied in.

The teachers were sitting on couches, in a circle. Some were gossiping over teacups, other had marking open beside them.

No one was looking her way. The window
overlooked the yard. It was open, just a
smidge. The dark clouds that had gathered
were starting to rain and heavy plops
dropped on the pane.

Where was the key?

54

She spotted it. There was a bookshelf on the right-hand side, with a neat row of keys hanging from hooks beside it. One of the keys was bigger than the others, black and old-fashioned, like the keyhole. It had to be that one.

But all of the teachers were between her and the key.

'Maybe this is a bad idea?' she whispered to Ryan.

He nodded. 'Going into restricted areas is, usually.'

But she was trying to be brave. So, she was going to have to do this, teachers or not.

She gripped her wrist nervously, and felt the shape of her bracelet under her jumper.

55

Was there anything magic could do? Not a
flood. Not again. But maybe a little drizzle?
Or a drip or two?

Evie backed away from the door. The
others huddled close.

'What are we going to do?' Isabelle asked.

'I haven't the foggiest,' Evie said.

Then, she grinned. 'That's it! Fog!' It was
perfect. 'If I use magic to make a fog in
there, a proper "can't see your hand in front
of your face" fog, then we can take the key
from right under their noses.'

Isabelle grinned and bounced excitedly.
'That's brilliant. You're a genius. Can you
do it?'

That was a very good question. She could

control water, and fog was made of water particles – they'd done the water cycle in Year 4 – so it *should* work. But sometimes magic worked for Evie, other times it was a right disaster! 'I can try,' she said.

Evie turned the bracelet on her wrist three times. Gold light twisted free and danced at the end of her hand. She crept back to the staff room door and peeked at the window. It was still raining hard. Good. In her mind she imagined the rain flowing into the room and turning gently into fog. Like clouds, or froths of candyfloss, or cotton wool. She tried to imagine exactly what she wanted the magic to do. *Fog,* she thought, *fog.*

The gold light twirled and danced into the staff room, headed for the window. It spread, like golden butterflies fluttering out. Some magic flew out of the window and turned the rain to thick white fog. Other bursts of light touched teacups and clouds of foggy tea drifted out of the mugs.

'What on earth?' one of the teachers said.

Pale fog poured in through the open window. Tea clouds drifted over the staff room. One last burst of magic landed on the coffee pot and a thick cloud of brown coffee-fog drifted upwards.

Oops.

It was getting hard to see now. The air was thick with beige fog.

'What's happening?' someone said from the midst of a particularly dense tea cloud.

'Strange atmospheric pressure!' the muffled voice of Mr Edwards, Head of Geography, replied.

'Climatic disturbance,' said Miss Linnet, Head of Science.

'Burnt dinners!' yelled Miss Campbell, Head of Food Tech.

Now was Evie's chance. The whole staff room was in cloudy turmoil. She raced in, keeping low to the ground. The fog was thick, and it smelled of hot drinks, but she surged through it towards the bookshelf. She bumped into a couch and banged against someone's shoe, making them yelp, but no one stopped her.

When she reached the shelves, she stood and patted the wall. Her fingertips landed on the rack of keys. She felt them quickly: little one, little one, big one! In seconds, she had the biggest key in her grasp.

She dropped down and crawled on all fours towards the door – at least, she hoped it was the door. It was tricky to see!

Yes, there it was. She could make out Ryan's face peeping in at her, low to the ground where the fog was lightest. She scurried faster, then was through.

Isabelle helped her up. 'Did you get it?' she asked.

Evie held up the key.

'Yay, Evie!' Isabelle said.

'Hush,' Ryan said, 'one of the teachers might hear you. Let's go.'

Evie took one last look at the staff room. The fog was beginning to clear and the teachers were looking at each other in befuddlement. It was probably time to make themselves scarce.

At the clocktower door, Evie slipped the key inside the lock and turned. She heard a smart click. She turned the handle and opened the door. It creaked, long and low, as it opened.

Before them was another staircase. This one was much narrower, barely room for them to go up in single file. The dark

wooden stairs had a thin layer of dust on
them – no one had been up here for a long
time. Which was odd. The caretaker had
heard people up here, hadn't he? The air
smelled musty and old. Evie shivered.

Was she really brave enough to do this?
She had to be. Ryan and Isabelle were both
watching her. She had to go first.

Evie stepped inside and began climbing. She could feel her heart thump in her chest.

And that's when she heard it.

A soft chuckle coming from above.

She froze. 'Did you hear that?' she hissed.

Isabelle was right behind her. She shook her head. 'I didn't hear anything.'

Had she imagined it?

Evie took another step, and another. The stairs turned, following the tower wall. It was grey-dark. The window above the clock was thick with grime. Hardly any light filtered in. She could see the back of the clock above them. Round cogs clicked, teeth to teeth, as the clock ticked.

Perhaps she had just heard the clock

ticking? Perhaps that was all it was?

Then, she heard it again. A chuckle, a laugh, echoing back and forth in the cramped darkness.

They were definitely not alone.

Chapter
6

Isabelle and Ryan had heard the laughter too. Evie felt Isabelle jump and Ryan stumble on the stairs.

'Was that a ghost?' Isabelle whispered.

'It can't have been, there's no such thing as ghosts,' Ryan replied.

Evie would have agreed – but a few

months ago she hadn't believed in magic either, and now she was using it to make tea clouds in the staff room. She didn't know what she believed.

There was only one thing for it. 'We have to investigate,' she said.

She felt the wall for a light switch, but found nothing. They would have to make do with the dim light from the grimy window above the clock.

Evie crept up the last few stairs. They were all in the small room at the top of the tower now. Her eyes were getting used to the gloom. What had made the noise? Shapes started to form, light grey on dark. As well as the clock mechanism, there were all kinds

of things stowed away in the tower. It must
be used as a store room for the school. It
was a messy store room though. The objects
were just thrown higgledy-piggledy on the
floor. It looked like the last hour of a jumble
sale, with everything tossed around in a

hurry. It smelled musty too, like old clothes.

'Hey!' Isabelle eased her aside and dropped to the ground. She lifted a black case. 'This is my clarinet. What's it doing up here?'

Evie saw a whiteboard rubber on the floor. And a scarf. It looked a lot like hers. But it couldn't be, could it? What was going on? There were single trainers, and a notebook and a sweater and a flask, and all kinds of things, in no order at all. How did they get up here?

Something darted across the room. It flashed in the corner of her eye, then was gone.

She spun around for a better look.

Another flash, in another corner.

Then another.

'What was that?' Isabelle gasped.

'What were those?' Evie corrected. Whatever it was up here, there were more than one.

Suddenly, a flurry of dark blue shapes flittered up above the clock mechanism. They whirred and swirled on fragile wings, fluttering higher.

'Bats!' Isabelle said, ducking and covering her hair.

No. Not bats. Evie recognised the long legs, the chatter and giggles of something that could do more harm than bats.

'Sprites!' she said.

As soon as she'd spoken, the whirling, whooping colony turned as one towards her. They chattered noisily about her head. One reached out and pulled her hair.

'Hey!' Evie yelled indignantly.

More sprites tugged and pulled her hair as they swirled around her. She ducked and tried to push them off. But they were too quick, and too many! They were laughing now, cheering each other on.

Eve felt someone grab her arm – Ryan! He pulled her towards the staircase. Isabelle was right behind them. They surged down the steps, taking them two at a time. At the bottom, Evie yanked open the door. The three tumbled through. She slammed it shut

73

behind her. Evie leaned against the wood, holding it closed with her back.

'How many of them were there?' Ryan asked.

'More than we've ever seen before,' Evie replied. They had come across mean little sprites on their adventures before, but usually only one or two. This time there were dozens!

'They've made a nest up there,' Ryan said, 'that must be what the caretaker heard. It was sprites going bump in the night!'

Evie pulled the key from her pocket and turned it firmly in the lock.

'What are you doing?' Ryan asked. 'We can't just leave them there.'

She looked at the key in her palm. They'd have to sneak it back into the staff room now, before the end of dinner time.

'Evie!' Ryan insisted.

'Maybe we should just leave them be? Let people believe it's a ghost, or mice, or something?' Evie said. She didn't like the idea of trying to get rid of so many sprites.

'They can't be trusted. You know they can't,' Ryan said. 'Remember what they did to your grandpa's garden?'

She did. They had ruined it. Grandpa had been so upset. It had taken them all working together to get rid of those two sprites – and that had only been two. There were dozens here.

75

Isabelle clamped her clarinet to her chest. 'And what about my clarinet, and all those other things? The sprites must have stolen them! We can't let them stay.'

Evie sighed. She slipped the key back into the lock. She had started out just trying to impress Isabelle and Ryan by being brave, but now they had a real job to do.

'We need a foolproof plan,' she said. There was no way she was walking back into a sprite colony without a very good idea indeed. 'We need to think of something even better than the time I invented using hollowed-out strawberries as ice cream cones. Even better than the time I told Lily that cartoons were the TV dreaming and she believed me. We need the best plan in the world ever.'

She glanced at the staff room door. Friendly chatter floated out. It didn't sound like any of the teachers would be moving for a while, so they had a bit of time.

'What will make the sprites leave?' Evie asked.

'We know they hate water,' Isabelle said.

'And,' Ryan nodded, 'every time we've seen them before, they've been hiding in shadows. I think they hate the light too.'

Evie counted off their suggestions on her fingers. As she looked down her eyes fell on the bracelet at her wrist. Of course! She could control water.

'We might have half a chance of beating them with magic,' she said. It was still raining outside – she could hear the pitter-patter on the roof above them. 'I can use the bracelet.'

Ryan looked excited. 'I can get torches. I saw two in the cleaner's cupboard when we put the mops away.'

Evie felt a little sheepish at the reminder of her accident earlier. But Ryan had a good point – there were torches they could use.

'So,' Isabelle said, 'the plan is, we all go running up there, lights blazing, magic sparking, and get all the rain that's going on outdoors to do it indoors instead?'

'That's right,' Evie agreed.

'There's just one problem.'

'What?'

'The window was shut. How's the rain going to get indoors?'

Hmm. She could move water, but she probably couldn't make it move through closed windows.

Isabelle read the look on her face. 'Don't worry,' she said. 'Ryan can handle the torches. You get ready with the magic. I'll open the window.'

They had a plan. They were ready to send the sprites on their way.

Chapter
7

Ryan disappeared past the staff room, back towards the ground floor and the torches. Evie and Isabelle were left on their own for a moment. They crouched down, with their backs against the wall, away from the eyes of teachers.

'Was it really an accident this morning?

The flood, I mean?' Isabelle asked.

What? Evie whipped her head round to
look at her friend. Was Isabelle serious?
'Of course it was an accident!'

Isabelle shrugged. 'I just feel right bad.
I knew you didn't want to audition. I'm
sorry I made you.'

'You didn't make me,' Evie protested.

'I kind of did,' Isabelle said with a sigh.
'I don't know when to take no for an
answer, my mum says.'

'But I didn't even say no,' Evie said. It
was true, she realised. She could have said
no, any time she wanted. But she hadn't.
She'd chosen not to. Evie realised that
there was a teeny, tiny part of her that

wanted to be up on stage.

She just had to be brave enough to admit it – and risk not getting a part, risk making a fool of herself.

There was no time to say so to Isabelle though, Ryan was back, out of breath and panting, and carrying two big torches, one in each hand.

'Did anyone spot you?' Isabelle asked.

'No. All clear,' Ryan gasped. He handed one of the torches to Isabelle.

'Evie, you open the door. Let me and Ryan go in. We'll use the torches to dazzle the sprites. I'll get the window open, then you use magic to make the rain pour down inside. OK?'

Everyone understood what they had to do. Evie gave a solid nod. Then she reached for the key, turned it and flung open the door.

As one, they charged up the stairs, clattering loudly to let the sprites know they were coming. Ryan and Isabelle both flicked on their torches – bright beams of light dazzled the space. As the white spotlight hit the walls, a whirlwind of sprites shrieked and flew up into the air from their hiding places in the rafters. Evie could see individual sprites caught in the glare; one had his hands up to cover his eyes, another bared his teeth in anger. Two of the sprites picked up a crate between them, wobbling as they lifted it. Then, they hurled it at Ryan's torch, desperate for the darkness.

Ryan ducked. The torches weren't going to hold them back for very long. Soon, their eyes would get used to the light and they'd be really cross!

Isabelle rushed over to the window. She had to open it if Evie was going to make it rain inside. She struggled to reach, with one hand still holding the torch.

'Evie, catch!' she cried and threw
the torch to Evie.

Evie caught it deftly, and held back the
gathering sprites with the beam. She had
to make sure Isabelle was safe and could
complete her mission. She rushed to Isabelle
and stood in front of her. Blue sprites
darted forwards, but she dazzled them
with light and they were forced back,
hissing as they went.

Behind her, she could hear Isabelle
pushing and shoving at the window catch.
Evie risked glancing over her shoulder, not
wanting to take her eyes off the sprites
for a moment.

Isabelle had climbed up on to the clock's
machinery and was straining hard with both
hands on the wooden window frame. Rain
smeared the pane outside. Evie was ready
to reach for her bracelet the second Isabelle
opened the window.

'Watch out!' Ryan called.

Evie spun back to face the sprites.
Ryan had shouted just in time. Three sprites
flew across the room, holding a heavy
book bag between them. They flew right
at Evie's head!

She ducked, and the sprites missed. She
heard them shriek in anger.

Ryan shone his beam at Evie's attackers,
but they were determined.

They wheeled about and dived again.
Evie's hands flew up to protect her head.

'I've got it!' Isabelle yelled.

Evie felt the freezing wet air rush
into the room through the open
window. Wind howled and whipped

88

up loose papers and rubbish.

Time for magic.

But the sprites had other ideas. The three carrying the book bag sped up. Evie crouched down to the ground. The bag missed her head, but hit her torch. It was dashed against the floor. She heard a smash and the light went out.

It was only Ryan's beam holding the sprites back. He dropped to Evie's side, waving the beam wildly, hoping to dazzle the attackers.

Above them, Isabelle pushed open the window as wide as it would go.

With a cry of rage, the biggest sprite hurled a black school shoe at Ryan.

89

He dashed it aside with his torch. But his beam of light went out.

They were in darkness.

Evie couldn't see anything for a second. She blinked hard, and then, she saw something that made her heart leap in her chest.

Dozens of sprites flew passed her, silently. Their wings made no sound. They held their arms outstretched, their fingers pinching and snapping.

They were flying at Isabelle.

When they reached her, they all grabbed at her, clinging on tight.

Isabelle was lifted right off her feet. Her legs kicked out. But the sprites held

90

fast, whisking Isabelle out of the open window into the sky beyond.

Isabelle was gone.

Chapter 8

'No!' Evie yelled in horror.

'Isabelle!' Ryan shouted.

But there was no Isabelle. The spot where she'd been moments before was empty. The sprites had flown her right out of the window.

Evie and Ryan dashed to the opening,

clambering on to the clock. They squished
side-by-side to see where the sprites had
taken Isabelle.

'Isabelle!' Evie cried.

'Evie!' The cry was faint, but it was

definitely Isabelle's voice. Evie could hear her yelling, over to their left. But the angle was all wrong to see exactly where she was. Somewhere on the roof, that was all she knew.

'I have to go and save her,' Evie said urgently. She gripped the bottom of the windowsill and started to pull herself up.

Two storeys below, the few children huddling on the yard looked like dolls. A ladder stretched from the window down the tower and flat along the roof to the narrow, railed walkway that ran above the guttering. It reminded her of the sort of ladders they had at the swimming baths. The rungs looked slippy in the rain.

'You can't go out there. The roof is only for adults, Miss Williams said,' Ryan cautioned.

'I agree. Which is why Isabelle shouldn't be out there. I'll be careful. I have to get her back, Ryan,' Evie said. She hoisted her knees up on to the sill and gently dropped one leg over the side. Ryan let go of her arm.

'OK,' he said, 'but I'm coming with you.'

Evie swung her other leg up over the sill. The cold air stung her face. She felt around with her toes until she felt the top rung of the ladder. She climbed down it carefully and lowered herself down to the roof. She followed the next ladder to the walkway and stepped on to it with a sigh. She'd made it,

the tricky part was done.

A handrail ran along the edge of the walkway. It was all made of metal the colour of over-chewed gum.

'Is it safe?' Ryan yelled from the window.

'Yes, but take it slow!'

Ryan was right behind her. She helped him find his feet on the walkway.

They had to tread very carefully. Despite the handrail, it felt like walking along the balance beam in gym class – but much higher up. Evie felt her tummy flutter with fear.

'Isabelle!' Ryan called.

This time there was no reply, even though they listened intently. All they could hear

was the wind, shrieks from the yard and the distant rumble of traffic.

The clock tower was set grandly in the centre of the long roof. At either end were chimney stacks that often had pigeons nesting in them. 'The sprites hate the rain,' Evie said. 'Maybe they're sheltering under a chimney.'

'But which one?' Ryan asked.

Evie saw at once what he meant. There were three school buildings in all. Evie and Ryan were on top of the main building, with the infants' building attached at an angle. There was also the block making up the dining hall and kitchen. The three buildings had been built at different times and they were a jumble of turrets, flat roofs, pointy roofs, air vents and chimneys. The maintenance walkway criss-crossed like a game of snakes and ladders over it all.

The sprites might be hiding Isabelle anywhere.

'Let's search,' Evie said.

They wasted no time at all. Ryan edged along the roof towards one chimney stack. Evie headed towards the other. She hoped and hoped that she'd peek around it and see Isabelle sheltering with the sprites, giving them a good telling-off.

In moments, she had balanced her way across the walkway, to the chimney. Rain dripped off its hood in rivulets. She peered

around the red brick stack, but there was no
one there. No sprites. No Isabelle.

She looked back towards the clock tower.
Had Ryan had better luck?

As she watched, Ryan appeared. He
caught her eye and shook his head. Isabelle

wasn't anywhere on this roof.

Evie was holding the handrail so tightly that her knuckles were pale. If Isabelle wasn't on this roof, had the sprites flown her away to the next roof, or the one after that, or even right out of the school and into the city?

No. Evie tried to squish down her panic. They wouldn't have been able to carry her very far. She was so much bigger than they were, and she was struggling, they'd get tired out quickly. What if they'd dropped her?

'We need to search the next roof,' Evie told Ryan as he made his way towards her. The next roof along was the dining room and kitchen. It wasn't attached to the main building. It was the newest of all the school buildings and had a flat roof, with lots of modern-looking machinery on it.

'OK,' he said doubtfully. 'I guess we can climb back into the clock tower and see if we can find a big ladder, or something like that, to climb up the other side.'

'There's no time,' she said. 'And I don't think anyone is going to let us climb up a ladder to the roof anyway, do you?'

Ryan shrugged. He moved around the chimney too, his feet inching their way ever so carefully so that they were both standing on the very edge of the roof, above the guttering. 'You might be right.

103

Well, actually, you are right. But we can't just leave Isabelle with the sprites.'

'Of course not,' Evie said. There was a gap, of just a metre or two, before the next roof began. Between the two buildings was a long drop, with the yard below. A plastic bag fluttered in the wind, trapped in the alleyway.

'We can't leave her,' Evie said with certainty. 'And we can't go back down.'

'Then,' Ryan sounded confused, 'then, what are we going to do?' he asked.

'We're going to jump,' Evie said.

Chapter 9

'Jump?' Ryan gasped. He peered over the edge, holding tight to the handrail. 'It's not a soft landing if we fall,' he said.

He was right. The yard was hard tarmac. It would definitely be a trip to casualty if they missed.

Not to mention all the trouble they'd be in

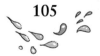

for climbing on the roof in the first place.

Was it the worst idea she had ever, ever had? Maybe.

Evie was about to agree with Ryan and try to come up with another plan, when something caught her eye. Something small and silver glistened on the roof opposite. Was it magic?

Evie leaned forward as far as she dared, in order to get a better look.

It was Isabelle's charm bracelet. It was curled on the rooftop beyond like a tiny jewelled snake.

They were definitely on the right track.

'We've got to be brave,' Evie said. 'We've both jumped much further before.'

'Yes,' Ryan said, 'but that was on the ground.'

There was a gap in the handrail to Evie's right. It was to give access to a ladder that ran down the side of the building. If she stood at the top of the ladder, she'd be able to jump. But she'd only have a few paces run-up, nowhere near what she'd have liked.

Could she make it?

'We've got to try,' Evie said. 'Isabelle needs us.'

She edged towards the gap, with Ryan at her side.

She rocked back and forth on her heels, swinging her body to find that extra lift. Ryan did the same thing.

'On three?' she said.

He nodded. They rolled forwards and back, forwards and back.

'One. Two. Three!' Evie yelled.

They took two hard paces, then launched up and out together. Evie stretched her front foot out, like a ballerina. She leaned into the jump, her arms pushing forwards. The gap opened up beneath her – it seemed that the next roof was miles away, not a metre.

And she landed, knees bent, on top of the dining hall.

Ryan clattered down beside her. She held his elbow to steady him. They had both made it safely.

Phew!

Evie dashed to the charm bracelet, which was in a puddle of water on the black tarred roof. 'This is definitely Isabelle's,' she said, showing it to Ryan. 'There's the unicorn. And the puppy.'

She put it in her pocket. She would be making certain that Isabelle got it back, safe and sound.

They were on top of the dining hall and kitchens now. The roof was mostly flat, with white boxes, the size of sideboards, dotted around. The boxes had fans in their middles, like cyclops eyes. They were the vents that took the hot air out of the kitchen.

'I hope she's here,' Ryan said. 'I do not want to have to jump back.'

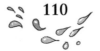

'Agreed. We'll find a different way down. Isabelle! Isabelle!'

A muffled cry came in reply. It came from the far side of the roof. They ran in that direction.

Right at the edge of the roof was a ventilation box that looked much worse than the others. It was battered and dingy. One of its sides was missing and bit of machinery had been thrown carelessly aside.

Ryan was the first to sprint towards it, but Evie wasn't far behind.

'Isabelle!' he yelled.

The cries were louder now, less muffled. Evie could hear high-pitched squeals too, as though there was a struggle going on.

111

From the gloom, a blue sprite darted. Its wings beat frantically. Then it rushed back into the darkness.

Evie was close enough to see what was happening. Isabelle was there, inside the box, wriggling fiercely! But she was surrounded by dozens of sprites. Some were trying to hold her legs, others her arms. Yet more tried to wrap a skipping rope

around her to keep her still.

They had already tied a scarf around her mouth to stop her yelling – not that it was really stopping her.

'Nnhurghh, nurrunghhuh,' Isabelle mumbled angrily.

'Hold her fast,' one of the sprites yelled.

'Hold her firm,' another added.

'Let her go!' Evie erupted.

A dozen heads whipped in her direction. A dozen mouths hissed.

Evie stepped back in alarm.

But then she saw Isabelle's eyes, wide and shining in the darkness. Her friend needed her.

They had to act, and fast.

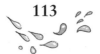

'Rain!' Ryan called. Evie had hardly noticed the heavy drops that had splashed on to her head and shoulders. She looked at the sky. The slate-grey clouds had rolled in again, heavy with rain.

'Use the rain!' Ryan said.

Evie reached for the bracelet at her wrist and turned it, once, twice, three times. The gold magic that streamed from it was piercingly bright under the gloomy clouds. The sprites covered their eyes in horror.

She raised her hands and thought, as clearly as she could, that the clouds should rain, rain, rain, right now! She imagined it falling like stair rods, like cats and dogs, lashing at the ground.

114

Magic raced upwards, dazzling her. It surged into the rain cloud. It was swallowed by the blackness.

Was that it?

Evie watched the sky anxiously. Had the magic failed?

Then she saw a flash and heard the low rumble of thunder. The few drops that had been falling became a shower, then a torrent. Soon the rain was bouncing off the roof, with a noise like stones thrown on gravel. Evie was soaked to the skin in seconds. Ryan's hair dripped and he wiped his eyes.

Inside the vent, the sprites cowered away from the rain, squealing and squeaking in alarm. Their grip on Isabelle weakened as they tried to press themselves away from the flood of water. Isabelle lunged forwards and pulled herself out of their grasp. She ripped the scarf from her face. 'Am I glad to see you two,' she said.

'I'm glad to see this downpour,' Ryan said. He leaned in and helped pull Isabelle clear.

The sprites didn't give chase. They hated getting wet more than anything.

Which meant that, if she was going to fix the school's sprite problem, they had to get very, very wet.

She turned the bracelet one more time. She concentrated as hard as she could on what she wanted the rain to do. The gold light

danced in the raindrops, pushing them this way and that. Then, the rain twisted and twirled and rained right into the vent, as though she had aimed a hose into it!

The first sprite to dash out flew straight up. The second flew north. The third flew

117

south. Soon, all the sprites flew from the school, headed out on the four winds, scattering.

Isabelle hugged Ryan and Evie tightly. 'You saved me,' she said in delight. Then, 'Eww, you're sopping wet,' she added.

They were. Evie could feel rain rolling down her neck. Ryan's normally spiky hair was flat as a pancake.

But magic would soon take care of that. She turned her bracelet and focussed as hard as she could.

The rain eased off to a light shower. The water on their clothes and in their hair sprang off in a fine mist that floated away.

Above them, the sun came out.

118

Then the bell for the end of dinner time
sounded.

Isabelle stepped forwards, then stopped.
'Er, guys,' she said. 'How are we going to
get down?'

Chapter 10

Evie looked around the roof. There was no way she was going to risk jumping back to the clock tower. They'd been lucky to make it the first time. There had to be a better way.

Ryan peered into the battered white box that Isabelle had been trapped inside.

'I think there's a way through here. They've pulled out the ventilation and made a hole. See?' he said. All the machinery that should have been inside the box was outside.

'I think this is how the sprites got into the school to steal all the things that have gone missing.'

Evie crouched and followed him into the vent. Right at the back was a spot darker than any other. A hole. It was just about big enough to crawl through. Ryan eased himself in. 'It slopes down,' he called back. 'It heads to the— wah!' Ryan's legs disappeared in a hurry, as he slipped and slithered down.

'Ryan!' Evie fell to her knees and looked

down into the darkness.

'It's OK,' Ryan's voice shouted up. She heard fumbling, and crashing, then a light flicked on. Ryan was standing in the cupboard off the hall that held all the gym equipment. He'd landed on a stack of tumble mats. 'It's safe,' he called up. 'You can come down.'

Evie and Isabelle were right behind him. Evie let herself slide, feet first, through the hole the sprites had made in the roof. She thumped down on to the mats and rolled clear for Isabelle to follow.

In seconds, they were out, and heading back to class. They were going to be late, no doubt about it. Evie picked up the pace,

123

without – quite – running in the corridors.

As they opened the Year 6 classroom door, Miss Williams glared at them. 'Where have you three been? The bell rang five minutes ago!'

Evie hung her head. 'I'm sorry, it's all my fault.'

'Somehow I doubt that,' Miss Williams said. 'I expect you all had something to do with it. It's a shame. I'd hate to give you an afternoon detention when the auditions have been rescheduled for straight after school.'

Oh no! Evie felt something she hadn't expected to feel at all at being told she couldn't audition – disappointment. It hadn't been Isabelle making her take part at all, she'd, deep down, wanted to do it. But she'd been scared that she'd fail.

She wasn't scared now.

'Please, miss,' Evie said. 'Don't give us detention today. If you have to give it to us, can we do it tomorrow, at break? You see, I want to audition. I want to be in the play.'

Miss Williams raised her eyebrows.
'Really? I hadn't thought … you didn't
seem …' Miss Williams stopped talking, and
gave a gentle smile.

'Well, in that case, you all have detention
… tomorrow. Now, take your seats.
Everyone, turn to chapter 3.'

At the end of the day, when the final bell
rang, Isabelle, Ryan and Evie went back
down to the music corridor. There was
a long line of people waiting to take part
in the auditions. They joined the back of
the queue.

Isabelle hugged her clarinet case. 'I hope I
get to be in the orchestra,' she said.

'I'm going to breakdance,' Ryan said
firmly. 'What about you? What will you
do, Evie?'

Evie reached into her pocket and pulled
out the charm bracelet she'd found on the
roof. She handed it back to Isabelle, who
slipped it on to her wrist.

'I'm going to do my best,' Evie said.
'There's a song I know all the words to.
I was singing it just this morning,
actually. Into the bathroom mirror,'
she giggled.

'What's it called?' Ryan asked.

'It's about being able to do anything –
with a little help from your friends,' Evie
said. 'It's pretty old, but I like it.'

Isabelle smiled and slipped her arm through Evie's. 'I know that one too. It's a good one.'

And they waited together until it was time to go in.

Evie

Full name: Evie Hall

Lives in: Sheffield

Family: Mum, Dad, younger sister Lily

Pets: Chocolate Labrador Myla and cat Luna

Favourite foods: rice, peas and chicken – lasagna – and chocolate bourbon biscuits!

Best thing about Evie: friendly and determined!

Isabelle

Full name: Isabelle Carter

Lives in: Sheffield

Family: Mum, Dad, older sister Lizzie

Favourite foods: sweet treats – and anything spicy!

Best thing about Isabelle: she's the life and soul of the party!

Ryan

Full name: Ryan Harris

Lives in: Sheffield

Family: lives with his mum, visits his dad

Pets: would love a dog …

Favourite foods: Marmite, chocolate – and anything with pasta!

Best thing about Ryan: easy-going, and fun to be with!

Evie's Magic Bracelet
Christmas

What's your perfect rainy-day activity?

What's your favourite item of clothing?

A. ❏ I love my raincoat!
B. ❏ My super-cosy onesie.
C. ❏ Snorkel and flippers.

Which animal is your fave?

A. ❏ Frogs – to match my froggie wellies.
B. ❏ Cats rule.
C. ❏ Penguins – I'm a water baby!

Your favourite colour is ...

A. ❏ Blue.
B. ❏ Orange.
C. ❏ Green.

The best thing to do with an umbrella is ...

A. ❑ Swirl it around while singing in the rain.
B. ❑ Leave it in the hallway!
C. ❑ Shelter under it while running for the bus.

I'm best at ...

A. ❑ Anything involving running and jumping.
B. ❑ Being creative.
C. ❑ Swimming!

The best thing about rain is ...

A. ❑ Getting wet!
B. ❑ Gives me the perfect excuse to stay home.
C. ❑ It's time for some indoor activities ...

Mostly A
Jumping in puddles!

Mostly B
Snuggled up with a book

Mostly C
Off to the swimming pool

Can you find all the words?

BRACELET   MAGIC
EVIE   CHARM
ISABELLE   CLOCKTOWER
RYAN   KEY
FRIENDS   SPRITES

G	Z	Y	V	M	J	X	B	S	C
S	Q	V	G	Y	D	R	M	E	L
E	L	L	E	B	A	S	I	T	O
T	S	K	K	C	R	M	T	I	C
M	E	D	E	Q	Y	Q	Y	R	K
Y	Z	L	N	C	A	H	N	P	T
D	E	D	I	E	N	S	W	S	O
T	E	G	P	S	I	S	Z	Y	W
W	A	V	C	H	A	R	M	U	E
M	J	D	I	F	F	Y	F	G	R
V	U	A	R	E	S	S	U	I	K

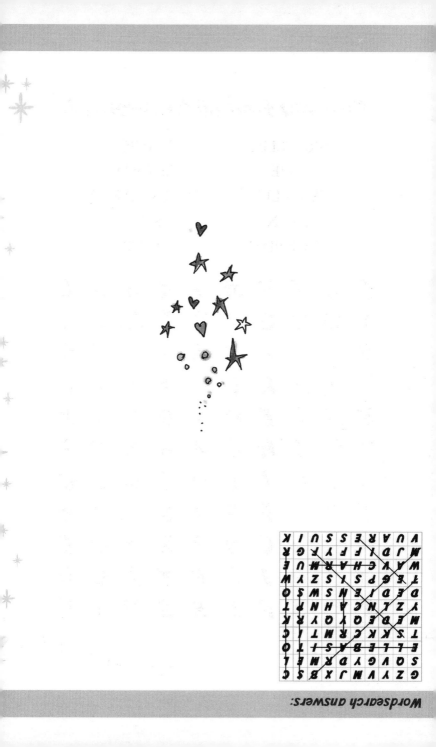

Jessica Ennis-Hill grew up in Sheffield with her parents and younger sister. She has been World and European heptathlon champion and won gold at the London 2012 Olympics and silver at Rio 2016. She still lives in Sheffield and enjoys reading stories to her son every night.

You can find Jessica on Twitter **@J_Ennis**, on Facebook, and on Instagram **@jessicaennishill**

Jessica says: *'I have so many great memories of being a kid. My friends and I spent lots of time exploring and having adventures where my imagination used to run riot! It has been so much fun working with Elen Caldecott to go back to that world of stories and imagination. I hope you'll enjoy them too!'*

Elen Caldecott co-wrote the Evie's Magic Bracelet stories with Jessica. Elen lives in Totterdown, in Bristol – chosen mainly because of the cute name. She has written several warm, funny books about ordinary children doing extraordinary things.

You can find out more at www.elencaldecott.com